Everyone Uses
Technology

Colleen Hord

rourkeeducationalmedia.com

Scan for Related Titles
and Teacher Resources

Teaching Focus:
Ending Punctuation- Have students locate the ending punctuation for sentences in the book. Count how many times a period, question mark, or exclamation point is used. Which one is used the most? What is the purpose for each ending punctuation mark? Practice reading these sentences with appropriate expression.

Before Reading:

Building Academic Vocabulary and Background Knowledge
Before reading a book, it is important to set the stage for your child or student by using pre-reading strategies. This will help them develop their vocabulary, increase their reading comprehension, and make connections across the curriculum.

1. *Read the title and look at the cover. Let's make predictions about what this book will be about.*
2. *Take a picture walk by talking about the pictures/photographs in the book. Implant the vocabulary as you take the picture walk. Be sure to talk about the text features such as headings, Table of Contents, glossary, bolded words, captions, charts/ diagrams, or Index.*
3. *Have students read the first page of text with you then have students read the remaining text.*
4. *Strategy Talk – use to assist students while reading.*
   - *Get your mouth ready*
   - *Look at the picture*
   - *Think…does it make sense*
   - *Think…does it look right*
   - *Think…does it sound right*
   - *Chunk it – by looking for a part you know*
5. *Read it again.*
6. *After reading the book complete the activities below.*

Content Area Vocabulary
Use glossary words in a sentence.

astronauts
endangered
engineers
inventions
scientists
solar

After Reading:

Comprehension and Extension Activity
After reading the book, work on the following questions with your child or students in order to check their level of reading comprehension and content mastery.

1. *What does technology do for people all over the world? (Summarize)*
2. *What is solar technology? (Asking questions)*
3. *Why are cameras needed to track endangered lions in India? (Infer)*
4. *What kind of technology entertains you? (Text to self connection)*

Extension Activity
Technology has changed the way people do things. With the help of an adult, make a list of the different ways people communicated with each other throughout history. Some ways to include on the list would be a letter, landline phone, or messenger pigeon. Create a timeline showing this technological advancement in communication. How do you think we will communicate with each other in the future? What other ways has technology changed life for people?

All around the world, people use technology every day.

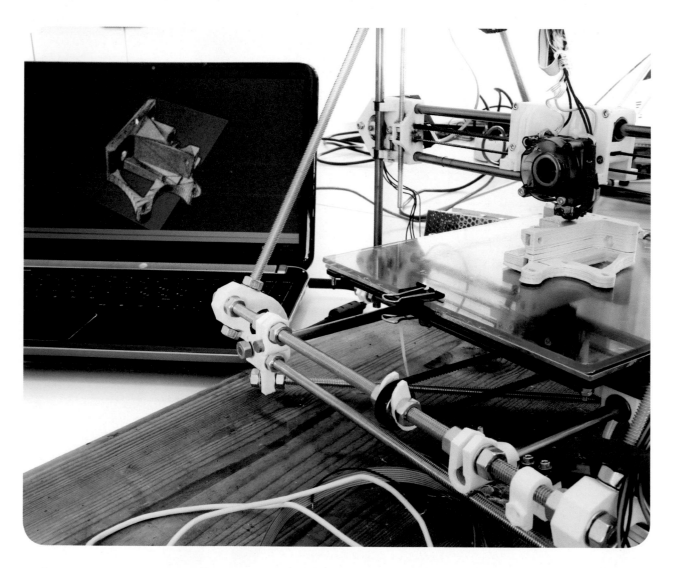

These **inventions** help people solve problems and make life easier.

Technology brings clean drinking water to villages in Africa.

Solar technology is used in Haiti and other places that need more electricity.

In India, people use camera technology to track **endangered** lions.

Technology also provides entertainment.

It is used to make movies and TV shows.

People everywhere use technology to communicate.

Someone in Spain can talk to someone on the opposite side of the Earth in New Zealand!

Technology is used to help people with injuries or disabilities.

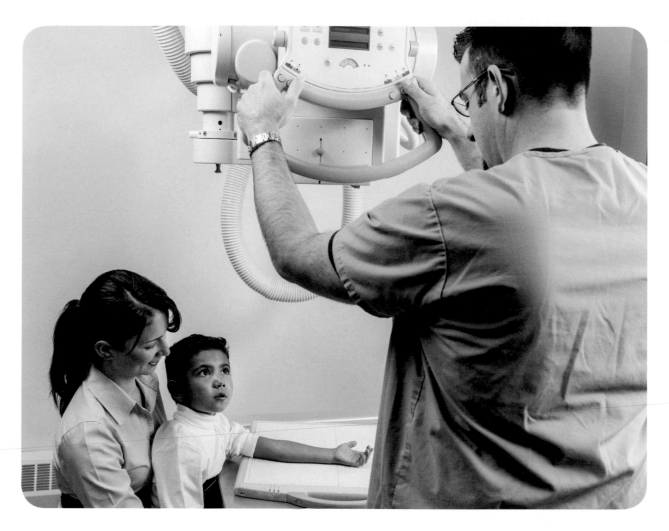

Scientists and **engineers** use technology to make machines and medicine that help people all over the world.

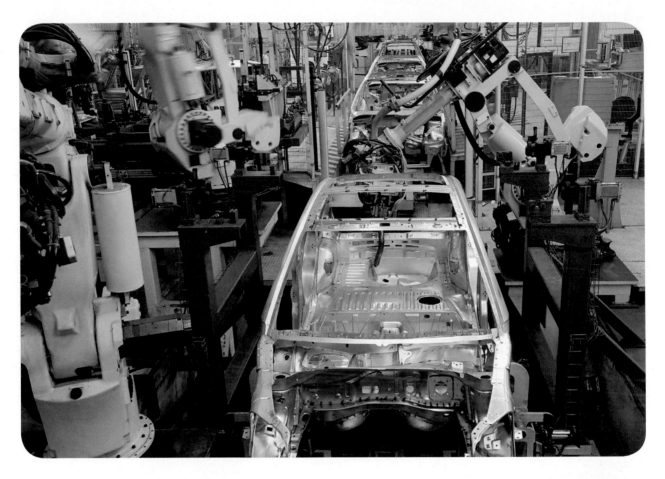

People in factories use technology to make the things we use every day. Factory robots in Tokyo help workers build things quickly and safely.

Robots can help do many things. Farmers in Ireland use robots to help milk their cows.

People who work on planes, trains, and ships use technology to keep travelers safe.

Technology even allows people to travel underwater!

Researchers use technology to live on the ocean floor for many days.

Technology isn't just here on Earth.

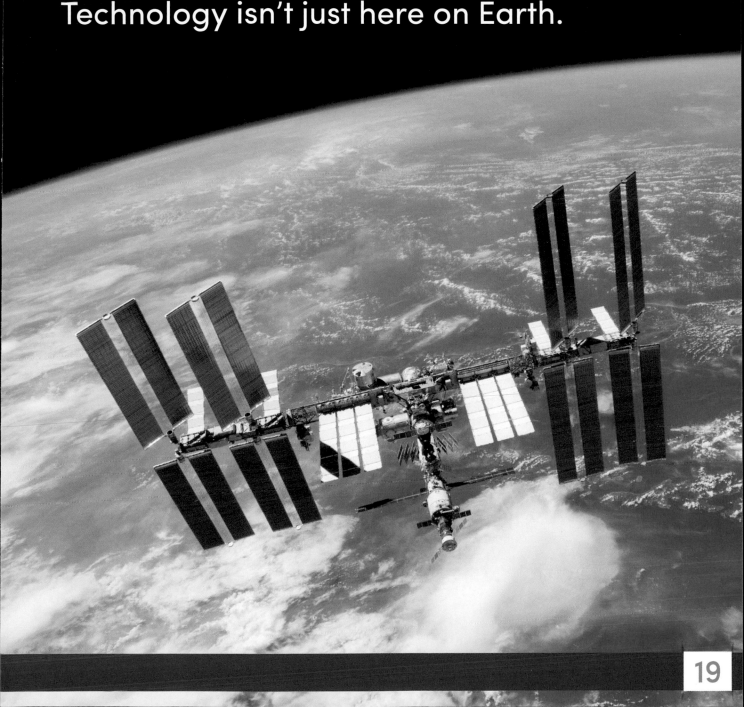

Astronauts from the United States, Japan, Russia, and other countries use technology to live and work in space together.

What technology have you used today?

Photo Glossary

 **astronauts** (ASS-truh-nawts): People who travel to space.

 **endangered** (en-DAYN-jurd): A plant or animal at risk of becoming extinct.

 **engineers** (en-juh-NIHRZ): People who are trained to design and build machines and structures.

 **inventions** (in-VEN-shunz): Products or devices someone makes up.

 **scientists** (SYE-uhn-tists): People who study nature and the world by testing and experimenting.

 **solar** (SOH-lur): Powered by energy from the Sun.

Index

astronauts 20

factories 14

inventions 4

machines 13

medicine 13

robots 14, 15

space 20

travel 17

Websites to Visit

www.nasa.gov

www.exploratorium.edu/explore

www.si.edu/Kids

About the Author

Colleen Hord is an elementary school teacher. She lives on six acres with her husband, chickens, ducks and peacocks. Writer's Workshop is her favorite part of her teaching day. When she isn't teaching or writing, she enjoys kayaking, walking on the beach, and gardening. She enjoys using technology that helps her keep in touch with her family and of course, the technology used to make books available for everyone, everywhere.

Show What You Know

1. What are some of the ways you use technology in your classroom?
2. How would your day be different without the use of technology?
3. Is it better for people or robots to make things and perform tasks? Explain your answer.

Meet The Author!
www.meetREMauthors.com

www.rourkeeducationalmedia.com

PHOTO CREDITS: Cover: © Yuri Arcurs, Csaba Toth; Title Page: © Pamela Moore; Page 3: © Rich Legg; Page 4: © Seraficus; Page 5: © africa924; Page 6: © Solar Electric Light Fund; Page 7: © Swisoot, Rethees; Page 8: © Christopher Futcher; Page 9: © bjones27; Page 10: © Christopher Futcher; Page 11: © Yobro10; Page 12: © Coke Whitworth - Associated Press; Page 13: © Christopher Futcher; Page 14: © Ric Aguiar; Page 15: © CHOMPOONUTBUANGERN; Page 16: © quavondo; Page 17: © dstephens; Page 18–19: © NASA; Page 21: © Monkey Business Images

Edited by: Keli Sipperley

Cover and Interior design by: Tara Raymo

Library of Congress PCN Data

Everyone Uses Technology / Colleen Hord
(Little World Everyone Everywhere)
ISBN (hard cover)(alk. paper) 978-1-63430-361-3
ISBN (soft cover) 978-1-63430-461-0
ISBN (e-Book) 978-1-63430-558-7
Library of Congress Control Number: 2015931697
Printed in the United States of America, North Mankato, Minnesota

Also Available as:

ROURKE'S
e-Books